# It's Raining, Yancy & Bear

Hazel Hutchins • Ruth Ohi

Annick Press Ltd.
Toronto · New York

©1998 Hazel Hutchins (text)
©1998 Ruth Ohi (art)
Designed by Ruth Ohi.

We acknowledge the support of the Canada Council
for the Arts for our publishing program.
We also thank the Ontario Arts Council.

**Cataloguing in Publication Data**

Hutchins, H.J. (Hazel J.)
  It's raining, Yancy & Bear

ISBN 1-55037-529-6 (bound)  ISBN 1-55037-528-8 (pbk.)

I. Ohi, Ruth. II. Title. III. Title: It's raining, Yancy and Bear.

PS8565 U826I87 1998    jC813'.54    C98-930183-4
PZ7.H87It 1998

The art in this book was rendered in watercolours.
The text was typeset in FZ Hand 21.

Distributed in Canada by:
Firefly Books Ltd.
3680 Victoria Park Avenue
Willowdale, ON
M2H 3K1

Published in the U.S.A. by Annick Press (U.S.) Ltd.
Distributed in the U.S.A. by:
Firefly Books (U.S.) Inc.
P.O. Box 1338
Ellicott Station
Buffalo, NY 14205

Printed and bound in Canada by
Friesens, Altona, Manitoba.

To best friends of all kinds...

H.J.H.

Early one morning, Bear feels a birthday coming on.

"Are you sure?" asks Yancy. "It's only been a month since your last birthday."

Bear is sure. Birthdays for Bear work differently than birthdays for Yancy.

"Hurrah!" shouts Yancy. He presents Bear with a balloon and dresses him in Yancy-overalls. On Bear's birthday Yancy and Bear change places.

"We'll have extra fun, because
today is Grandfather's garden-planting
day," Yancy announces, climbing into
Bear's sailor suit. Bear adds a final
touch and a big thank-you.

Yancy flies like an airplane as Bear races downstairs. There they both stop. Grandfather is looking out the window. Outside it is raining. Hard. Much too wet to plant a garden.

It is difficult to tell which of the three is most disappointed.

Grandfather looks down at Bear and Yancy and the balloon.

"Not a very good day for a birthday, I'm afraid," he says, gathering them into his lap.

Something has stuck to the balloon. It is a page from the newspaper Mother brought in before she left for work.

"'Children's Play at Museum,'" reads Grandfather aloud. "Maybe that would be just the thing to rescue someone's special day."

The rain comes down heavily on the way to the bus stop. Bear is kept busy holding tight to Grandfather with one hand and Yancy with the other. Like a great friendly creature the bus pushes through the rain to meet them.

Inside it is warm and
bright. Bear and Yancy
look out the windows at
the wonderful splashing of
traffic and the bouncing
flow of umbrellas.

Grandfather sighs. The
first happy seeds of
spring he was going to
plant today are so small
they would just float
away with all this rain.

The museum is a big, big building. Inside, escalators and stairs seem to go up forever and people are going every which way. Bear can see all sorts of things beyond the glass doors.

"This is the kind of museum where we are not allowed to touch anything," explains Grandfather. "But we can look around a little before the play begins."

Bear doesn't want to stand and look for long, but he wants to see everything. He wants to see the suits of armour and the long house and the Chinese burial horses.

He drags Grandfather
all the way to the top of
the building to see
the Egyptian
mummies.

He drags Grandfather all the way to the bottom of the building to see the dinosaurs. He can't decide which he likes best—dinosaurs or mummies or long house.

Yancy likes the dinosaurs best, but the escalators are a lot of fun too.

"You've been up and down past
me four times," laughs an attendant.
"Is it still raining outside?" asks
Grandfather.

She nods. Grandfather gives up
all hope of garden-planting.

When it is time, they go to the theatre. Grandfather sits in one seat—he is so tired he begins to drift off to sleep even as the lights go down. Bear and Yancy sit in another. At least, *most* of the time Bear and Yancy sit together.

Some of the time, Bear joins in with the action on stage. The play is about hunting for dinosaur bones and Bear takes his part very seriously. No one really minds. One person thinks he does such a good job that afterwards she gives him a coupon to trade for something small at the gift shop.

"Did you like the play?" asks the attendant.

"It seems I missed a few key parts," says Grandfather.

Bear spends a long time going up and down the aisles in the gift shop. Yancy understands why. Suddenly he sees something that will be perfect. He sends special thought waves to Bear.

"There, Bear! Over there!"

Bear sees what Yancy has spotted.

When Mother comes home that evening she finds supper on the table and Grandfather, Yancy and Bear looking out the window. Bear and Yancy race to give her a hug.

"Did you have a good time today?" asks Mother.

"Yes, indeed," says Grandfather. "And we're going to have another good time in just a few minutes, I hope."

The three of them go back to the window. They are waiting for the rain to let up...just a little.

When at last it slows, they hurry into their rain clothes and go out into the garden. Bear opens the bag he and Yancy brought from the gift shop, the bag of big, flat sunflower seeds that not even all this rain will wash away. Together with Grandfather, they plant the first seeds of spring.

Sometimes rainy days make the
best birthdays of all.